Bea
the Buddha Day
Fairy

Join the **Rainbow Magic Reading Challenge!**

I the story and collect your fairy points to climb the
Reading Rainbow at the back of the book.

This book is worth 1 star.

To Lara, who is wise and kind

Special thanks to Rachel Elliot
With thanks to Inclusive Minds
for connecting us with their
Inclusion Ambassador network, and in
particular to Zainab M Ahmad
for their input

ORCHARD BOOKS

First published in Great Britain in 2021 by The Watts Publishing Group

1 3 5 7 9 10 8 6 4 2

© 2021 Rainbow Magic Limited.
© 2021 HIT Entertainment Limited.
Illustrations © 2021 The Watts Publishing Group Limited.

HiT entertainment

A CIP catalogue record for this book is available from the British Library.

ISBN 978 1 40836 236 5

Printed and bound in Great Britain by Clays Ltd, Elcograf S.p.A

MIX
Paper from
responsible sources
FSC® C104740
www.fsc.org

The paper and board used in this book are made from wood from responsible sources

Orchard Books
An imprint of Hachette Children's Group
Part of The Watts Publishing Group Limited
Carmelite House, 50 Victoria Embankment, London EC4Y 0DZ

An Hachette UK Company
www.hachette.co.uk
www.hachettechildrens.co.uk

Bea
the Buddha Day
Fairy

By Daisy Meadows

ORCHARD

www.orchardseriesbooks.co.uk

Fairyland
Palace

Festival Island

The Golden River

High Street

Rachel's
House

TIPPINGTON
TOWN

Jack Frost's
Ice Castle

Jack Frost's Festival Tent

WETHERBURY

Kirsty's House

Jack Frost's Spell

Ignore Eid and Buddha Day.
Make Diwali go away.
Scrap Hanukkah and make them see –
They should be celebrating me!

I'll steal ideas and spoil their fun.
My Frost Day plans have just begun.
Bring gifts and sweets to celebrate
The many reasons I'm so great!

Contents

Chapter One
Waiting for Rachel

It was a sunny morning in Wetherbury, and Kirsty Tate had been bouncing around her house since she had woken up. Her best friend, Rachel Walker, was coming to stay for the weekend. Kirsty skipped into the kitchen, twirled around three times and gave her dad a big hug.

"Calm down," said her dad, laughing and hugging her back.

"I can't," Kirsty said, glancing at the wall clock. "Rachel will be here any minute."

"It's been quite a long time since you last saw each other," said her mum. "I expect you'll have lots to talk about."

Kirsty smiled. Her mother had no idea that the girls had seen each other not long ago. They were secretly friends with the fairies, and when Jack Frost had stolen four magical objects that belonged to the Festival Fairies, Rachel and Kirsty had promised to help get them back.

On the night of the new moon, they had been transported to Fairyland and had saved Elisha the Eid Fairy's pelita lamp from Jack Frost and his mischievous goblins. Altogether, they had now rescued three magical objects. However, Bea the Buddha Day Fairy's special candle was still missing, and today was Buddha Day. Time was running out.

A car door slammed outside and Kirsty raced to the door. Was it her best friend at last?

"Yes!" she exclaimed.

Rachel was running up the path towards her, followed by Mr and Mrs Walker. The girls shared a happy hug.

"Let's go upstairs and unpack your bag," said Kirsty.

While their parents went to have a cup of tea, the girls hurried up to Kirsty's room. Rachel shut the door behind her and leaned against it, smiling.

"Happy Buddha Day," she said. "I've been thinking about Bea all morning."

"Me too," said Kirsty. "Wasn't our adventure with Elisha exciting?"

"Yes, and I was so surprised when you turned up at my window," said Rachel, laughing as she remembered. "Thank goodness we found the pelita lamp. I just hope that we can find Bea's magical candle too."

She started to unpack her bag. Kirsty always kept one of her drawers empty, ready for Rachel's visits.

"I hope Bea arrives soon," said Kirsty, longingly. "Buddhists all over the world are celebrating the birth of Buddha today. It's called the Vesak Festival. I can't bear to think of Jack Frost spoiling that, just so he can create his own festival."

"Don't forget what Queen Titania told us," said Rachel. "The magic will find us."

"So we don't have to go looking for it," Kirsty added. "OK, what shall we do this morning?"

The door opened and Mrs Tate came in, holding a leaflet.

"This has just arrived," she said. "I thought you two might be interested. There's a new Buddhist temple on the outskirts of Wetherbury. They're having an open day today, and they have invited everyone to go along and learn something about Buddhism. Would you like to go?"

The girls shared a delighted smile and nodded. Perhaps the magic was already at work!

"Do you think Bea has arranged this?" Kirsty asked as soon as her mother had left the room.

"I don't know," said Rachel. "But it sounds like a great way to understand more about Buddhism."

The girls ran down the stairs, thrilled to think that another magical adventure might be on the way. They made a little picnic of sandwiches, hard-boiled eggs, carrot sticks and blueberries, and divided the packets between their rucksacks.

"Let's go on our bikes," Kirsty suggested.

Luckily, Rachel had brought her bike to Wetherbury. Mrs Walker took it off the rack on the back of the car, while the girls filled their bottles with cool, fresh water.

"Be home in time for tea," said Mrs Tate.

"We will," called Rachel and Kirsty as they rode off down the street. "Goodbye!"

They chatted as they pedalled past the little shops and the church, towards the edge of the village. It was lovely to be together again, sharing stories and jokes. Soon they had left the houses behind.

Hedges rose up on either side of the lane. They stopped and perched on a wooden stile to have their picnic.

"It can't be much further," said Kirsty, checking the leaflet that her mum had given them. "Yes, I think it's around the next bend in the road."

When they had eaten, Rachel jumped back on to her bike, sped down the lane and peeped around the bend.

"Yes, I can see it," she called.

Kirsty whizzed after her.

"WHEEEE!" she shouted, sticking her legs out and letting the bike freewheel.

She skidded to a stop beside Rachel, giggling. In a break in the hedgerow, an arched iron entrance had the words 'Wetherbury Buddhist Temple' written in gold letters. Through the archway was a long, low building made of honey-coloured stone. The girls parked their bikes and walked along a winding path towards the front door.

Chapter Two
The Glowing Bowl

The path wound around rose bushes, jasmine plants and knobbly old trees. When Rachel and Kirsty reached the front door, it was opened by a young woman, who put her palms together and gave a small bow.

"Welcome to the Buddhist Temple," she

said, smiling. "My name is Emma."

"I'm Kirsty and this is Rachel," said Kirsty. "Happy Buddha Day."

"Thank you," said Emma. "Please come in."

The girls followed her inside. The entrance hall was light and airy, and there was a delicious scent of flowers.

"Do you live here?" Rachel asked.

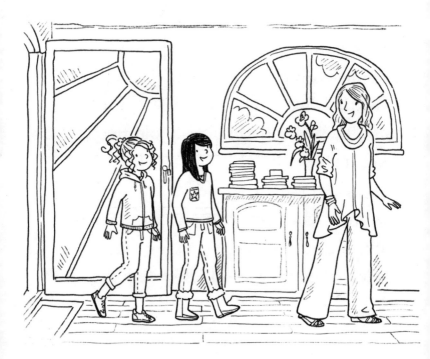

"No," said Emma. "But I spend a lot of time here. I'm one of a group of people who follow the teachings of a wise man called the Buddha. I hope you'll understand a bit more about him and us after your visit today."

"Is this the Buddha?" asked Kirsty, pausing by a statue.

Emma nodded. It was a simple stone figure of a man sitting cross-legged with his eyes shut. There was a candle on each side.

"It makes me feel peaceful," said Rachel.

"Me too," said Emma. "In his life, the Buddha searched for wisdom and understanding. On Buddha Day, we celebrate his life and the things he taught. All over the world, Buddhists will be meditating, volunteering for charity work and making lanterns and beautiful art."

The girls exchanged a worried glance. They knew that as long as Bea's special candle was missing, Buddhist celebrations everywhere were in danger of being spoiled.

Emma led Rachel and Kirsty into a large room with white walls and oak beams. Inside was a larger, golden statue of the Buddha. There were low tables around the statue, with beautiful items on each one.

"Here are some special things that we

use to help us clear our minds and relax," Emma said, showing them a small copper dish filled with water. "This is one of our singing bowls."

She picked up a little mallet and ran it around the outside rim of the bowl. It made a clear, bright sound, and the water inside started to bubble and dance, fizzing into droplets and little waves.

Next, Emma showed them a prayer wheel. It was a metal cylinder on a wooden spindle.

"There is a mantra carved into the metal," she explained. "A mantra is a saying that has a special meaning, like a prayer. Spinning the cylinder around and around sends your prayer out into the universe."

"Is this a necklace?" asked Kirsty, picking up a string of beads.

"They are prayer beads," said Emma. "There are one hundred and eight beads. Buddhists say mantras over and over again to help them banish negative thoughts. The beads help us to keep count and focus the mind."

A chime rang out.

"That must be another visitor," said

Emma. "I hope you'll spend some time with us today. Around the temple you'll find people telling stories about the Buddha, lessons in how to meditate and some vegetarian food for you to try. If you're still here later, maybe you could join in the march and prayer gathering."

"We'd love to," said Rachel.

Emma pressed her palms together and gave another small bow. Then she went to greet the new visitor. Rachel and Kirsty knelt down beside the low

table. There were many singing bowls of different colours and sizes.

"Which is your favourite?" Rachel asked.

Kirsty leaned over to look at them all, and gasped.

"Look at that one at the back," she said in a low, thrilled voice.

The little bowl was glowing with a light that the girls had seen many times before.

"Magic!" said Rachel.

Chapter Three
Bea Appears

The glow grew brighter, and the girls had to cover their eyes. When the light faded, they saw Bea the Buddha Day Fairy inside the singing bowl.

"Bea!" exclaimed Kirsty. "We've been hoping we would see you soon."

The little fairy was sitting with the

soles of her feet pressed together and her legs in a diamond shape. She lifted her head, fluttered her wings and smiled at Rachel and Kirsty.

"Is that a yoga pose?" asked Rachel.

"It's Butterfly Pose," said Bea. "It helps me to feel calm, even though my magical candle is still missing."

She slowly unfolded herself and stood up. She was wearing a red silk dress, decorated with delicate blue and yellow flowers. Red flowers shaped like stars were tucked into her dark hair. Her shoes were red and gold, and her gossamer wings were the blue of a summer sky. The golden belt around her waist glistened like a candle flame.

"I'm glad to find you here at the Buddhist Temple," she said. "I've followed the goblins here. Jack Frost is angry because you have taken back all the other things they stole from us. He has sent them here to spoil the celebrations and upset us all."

At that moment, the girls heard loud, slapping footsteps and squawking voices.

"That's the goblins," said Kirsty in alarm. "Where can we hide?"

There was a table at the back of the room, draped with an embroidered cloth. Rachel and Kirsty dived underneath it, and Bea followed them. They were only just in time. Five goblins burst into the room, wearing tracksuits and caps, and arguing in loud, rough voices.

"We just have to find things that we can use to celebrate Frost Day," said the first goblin. "The candle will do the rest."

Bea peeped out from under the cloth

and saw a short
goblin waddle
towards the
singing
bowls. In
his cupped
hands
he was
cradling a
small, ivory-
coloured candle in

a holder of red lotus petals.

"That's my candle," Bea whispered. "It's so close! There must be a way to get it back."

As she spoke, the goblin touched one of the singing bowls with the candle. At once, the burnished copper turned a dull green. Another goblin picked up the mallet and ran it around the outside of the bowl. Instead of the beautiful sound the girls had heard earlier, the room echoed with shrill laughter.

"They've turned it into a cackling bowl," said Bea, her eyes full of sadness. "My candle will change anything it touches to suit the person holding it."

"We have to get it back before they spoil everything," said Rachel.

The goblin started banging the candle against all the special things on the low tables. Prayer beads became hailstones and prayer wheels turned into blue lightning bolts.

"I hope they don't melt," said Kirsty.

Bea shook her head.

"My candle is very clever," she said. "It has locked the ice into those shapes."

The goblin had run out of things
to change. He looked up at the large,
golden statue of the Buddha.

"Oh no, he can't," cried Rachel.

As soon as the candle touched the

statue, a flicker of blue passed over the gold, and a sheen of frost appeared. The Buddha's gentle smile was replaced by a spiky scowl. A beard sprang from his chin, and his eyes grew thin and mean.

"They've turned it into a statue of Jack Frost," said Kirsty, horrified. "We have to stop them before Emma sees it."

"If this happens all over the world, Buddha Day will be a disaster," said Bea.

"We'll stop them right here and get your candle back," said Rachel. "I promise."

The room grew colder as more and more objects were changed to fit the Frost Day theme.

"I'm bored now," said the short goblin. "Let's find something else to mess up."

The goblins scampered out, slamming the door behind them, and the girls crawled from their hiding place. Bea fluttered into the air.

"Quickly, let's follow them," she said.

At that moment, the door opened and Emma came in. Rachel and Kirsty jumped in front of the changed statue, and Bea dived underneath Rachel's hair.

37

Emma looked puzzled, and the girls held their breath. Had she noticed the frosty statue, and had she seen Bea?

Chapter Four
A Scary Book

"Goodness, it's cold in here," Emma said. "Rachel and Kirsty, would you come and listen to some stories about the life of the Buddha? My good friend Ben is giving a reading."

Phew! Rachel and Kirsty nodded, and followed Emma out of the room.

"That was close," said Kirsty in a low voice. "Look out for goblins."

"After the march later, there will be a ceremony called Bathing the Buddha," said Emma. "We will pour water over the golden statue to celebrate new beginnings."

Rachel and Kirsty shared an alarmed glance. The golden statue was now a sculpture of Jack Frost!

Emma led them to a small, cosy room where a man was reading aloud from a large old book on his lap. A few other people were already there, listening, but there were no goblins. Rachel and Kirsty sat down and crossed their legs.

"Next, I will tell you about how Siddhartha Gotama became the Buddha," said Ben, turning the page.

"Leaving his kingdom behind, Siddhartha became a wandering monk. He grew spiky hair and a frosty beard to show that he was better than everyone else—

Hold on. This isn't right!"

Ben riffled through the pages, but every word seemed wrong.

"Snow . . . cold heart . . . unkindness?" he murmured. "Someone is playing tricks and swapping books."

Rachel and Kirsty shared a knowing glance. The goblins must have touched the book with their candle.

"Perhaps you would like to look around

the temple while I find another copy,"
said Ben, smiling around at the group.

People made their way out of the room.
Soon, Rachel and Kirsty were the only
ones left.

"Shall we go and look for the goblins?"
Rachel asked.

"In a minute," said Kirsty. "I'd like to
look at the book."

She picked up the
heavy volume.
On the cover,
instead of
the Buddha,
there was a
picture of
Jack Frost
standing
outside his castle.

"He wants everything to be about him," said Rachel. "He's so vain."

Suddenly, the picture of Jack Frost lunged forwards. Kirsty screamed and dropped the book. His face had filled the cover.

"Don't be rude!" the picture yelled.

Then a hand reached out through the cover.

"That's the real Jack Frost," said Rachel with a gasp. "He's climbing out of the book!"

Jack Frost jumped into the room, shook a shower of snow from his cloak and sneered at the girls.

"You've lost," he said. "My frosty powers will turn everything Buddhist to ice, and they will have to celebrate Frost Day and ME."

"You can't just steal a whole festival and make it yours," Kirsty exclaimed.

Jack Frost glared at her and gave a low hiss.

"I can do whatever I want," he replied. "You think you're so clever, tricking my

goblins and getting your magical objects back. But this time you're up against me. I have hidden the candle in a place where you will never find it."

He stepped towards them, and the air seemed to grow colder.

"What are you going to do?" Kirsty asked.

"I'm going to use the candle's magic to change this place into a Frost Temple," said Jack Frost with an unpleasant chuckle. "It's perfect for my celebrations!"

He waved his wand and there was a

disturbing crackling sound. Ice crusted the
walls and icicles sprang from the lights.

"Soon those silly, gentle Buddhists will
be bathing statues of me," he yelled.

Then he whipped around and left the
room, his cloak swirling behind him.

Bea fluttered out from underneath
Rachel's hair.

"Please can we start searching straight
away?" she said. "My candle must be

here somewhere if Jack Frost is using it to make these changes. I have to get it back."

"It'll be quicker if we can fly," said Rachel.

Bea tapped her wand on her palm, and then blew on her hand. A cloud of glimmering fairy dust puffed up into the air and sprinkled down on to the girls. They felt their skin tingling as the magic

started to work. They shrank to Bea's size in a haze of sparkles.

"Hello, wings!" said Rachel, twirling up into the air.

Suddenly, the little room seemed like a vast chamber. Kirsty fluttered her own translucent wings and swooped over to the door.

Chapter Five
Ignoring Jack Frost

The three fairies rose up and glided through the open door and across the hallway. Staying close to the ceiling, they went into the first room. The statue of Jack Frost was still there, the bowls were still green and the beads were still frozen. The walls were thick with ice, and several visitors were shivering.

"I don't remember the Buddha looking like that," said one lady, looking up at the sculpture.

Emma walked in and saw the ice sculpture. To Rachel and Kirsty's surprise, she stayed completely calm and smiled at the visitors.

"We seem to be having a few difficulties with the temperature," she said. "If you will step outside, we would love to lead you in a Buddhist meditation in the warmth of the sun and the beauty of nature."

As soon as the visitors had left the room, the fairies zoomed around and checked every nook and cranny.

"No candles," said Rachel. "We'll keep looking."

They swooped out of the room and searched the hallway. There were many more rooms to be explored, and the fairies looked carefully in each one. They found more Buddha statues that had changed to Jack Frost. They found prayer wheels, singing bowls and prayer beads, which had all been changed to suit

Frost Day. But Bea's magical candle was nowhere to be seen.

The fairies flew back to the hallway and landed on a high shelf.

"What if we never find it?" asked Bea in a little voice.

She sat down and dangled her legs over the edge. Rachel and Kirsty squidged close on either side of her.

"We won't stop until we get your candle back," Kirsty promised.

"However long it takes," Rachel added.

"We are your friends," said Kirsty. "That means that we are here to help you, even when things are hard and scary."

"Thanks, you two," Bea said. "I feel better. Let's keep looking."

"Wait," said Rachel in an urgent whisper.

She pointed at the door. Jack Frost strode in, and

the five goblins scurried after him. He hadn't spotted the fairies.

"These Buddhists are silly," he grumbled. "I've turned them out of their building and spoiled all their things. Why don't they care? Why aren't they shouting and arguing? They just smile and find something else to do. They're getting on my nerves."

"Jack Frost can't bear to be ignored," said Kirsty.

"That's it!" said Rachel. "Jack Frost likes to see that he's bothering people. If we pretend not to notice him, he might get cross."

"I'm not sure I want him to get cross," said Kirsty.

But Bea was nodding eagerly.

"When people get cross, they don't

think about what they are saying," she said. "If we annoy Jack Frost, he might start yelling and give us a clue about where the candle is."

It was a bit scary to think of Jack Frost yelling at them. But if he yelled something helpful, it might be worth it.

"We'll need to be human again," said Kirsty.

They floated down to the ground, and Bea returned Rachel and Kirsty to their

usual size. The little fairy popped herself into Kirsty's pocket. Jack Frost was still standing in the doorway.

"Come on," said Rachel.

The girls linked arms and walked towards the door. Their hearts thumped, but they held their heads up high.

"You'll never find that candle," hissed Jack Frost as they passed him.

Rachel and Kirsty took no notice. Jack Frost frowned.

"Hey!" he shouted. "You and that silly fairy have lost. Her candle is mine for ever."

Rachel and Kirsty saw Ben and Emma leading the meditation class. They went to join in, and Jack Frost and the goblins followed them.

"Look downwards," Ben was saying.

"Notice your breath as the air goes out of your body and joins the space around you."

"The Festival Fairies are going to be sorry that they refused to help me," said Jack Frost behind them.

Rachel and Kirsty just breathed. Jack Frost seethed.

"Why aren't you listening to me?" he hissed.

"Keep thinking about your breath," said Ben. "If your mind wanders to something else, just say to yourself, 'thinking', and go back to focusing on your breath."

Ben kept talking, and Rachel and Kirsty felt their breath slowing down. One by one, their worries slipped away. After a few minutes, they weren't even thinking about Jack Frost and the goblins behind them. In Kirsty's pocket, Bea was doing the same thing.

When the meditation ended, the girls shared a relaxed smile. Then they turned and stared in amazement.

Jack Frost and the goblins were sitting

in Butterfly Pose. They all had their eyes shut, and one of the goblins was humming.

"I can't believe it," said Rachel, rubbing her eyes. "Jack Frost is . . . meditating."

Chapter Six
Jack Frost Tries Kindness

"I never thought I'd see this," said Kirsty.

"Maybe this is the perfect moment," Bea whispered. "For once, he's not shouting or arguing. Perhaps he'll try listening."

The girls sat down in front of Jack Frost, and he slowly opened his eyes.

"Do you like the way you feel right now?" Rachel asked.

Jack Frost's eyebrows rose up in surprise. Then he nodded.

"That's the feeling that you will take away from people if you spoil the Buddha Day celebrations," said Kirsty.

Bea popped her head out of Kirsty's pocket.

"We Festival Fairies want everyone to feel peace, caring and happiness," she said. "Not only humans, but fairies and goblins too."

"I just wanted to have a festival day," said Jack Frost.

For once, he spoke in a quiet voice.

"Frost Day can work," Bea promised. "I will help you, and so will the other Festival Fairies. But it won't happen if you are selfish and always put yourself first. Happiness comes from living a life that is helpful to everyone and making kind choices."

"Like what?" asked Jack Frost.

"Like giving Bea back her candle," said Rachel. "If you did that, you would feel even more amazing."

Jack Frost thought for a moment. Then he reached into his cloak and pulled out Bea's cream-coloured candle in its red lotus petal holder.

Rachel and Kirsty gasped. Was Jack Frost really going to make a kind choice?

"Here," he said, holding it out to Bea.

As soon as Bea touched it, the candle shrank back to fairy size. She smiled.

"Thank you with all my heart," she whispered. "When you've worked out what you want Frost Day to celebrate, I promise I will help you to organise it."

Jack Frost took a deep breath . . . and smiled. The goblins stared at him and their mouths dropped open.

"I want that feeling again," he said in a louder voice. "What next?"

"How about doing something nice for the goblins?" Kirsty suggested.

Jack Frost took out his wand and waved it towards the goblins, who ducked. There was a crackle of blue magic, and then each goblin was holding a frozen ice sculpture of a candle.

"These are to say thank you," said Jack Frost.

Big smiles spread over the goblins'

knobbly faces, and Jack Frost's smile grew bigger.

"That feels good too," he said, sounding surprised.

"Thanks," said the first goblin.

"Mine's really cold," said another.

"And slippery!" added a third. "EEEK!"

The candle shot out of his hands like a rocket and hit another goblin in the tummy.

"*UFFF!*" said the goblin, sitting down

in a patch of dandelions.

Jack Frost threw back his head and cackled with laughter.

"You're right, doing things for others really does make me feel better," he said. "That was the funniest thing I've seen all day! I'm going to give the goblins more things so they can make me laugh."

Still chuckling, he raised his wand. He and the goblins vanished in a puff of blue smoke.

"I don't think Jack Frost quite

69

understands the idea of making kind choices yet," said Kirsty.

"No," said Bea. "But it's good that he tried!"

Her candle was cupped in her hands, and Rachel and Kirsty exchanged a happy smile.

"We're really glad that you got the candle back," said Kirsty. "Now the Buddhist Temple can go back to normal, and Buddha Day is saved."

"It's all thanks to you," said Bea. "The Festival Fairies will never forget what you have done for us. But now it is time for me to take the candle back to Festival Island, and for you to join in the march and prayer gathering."

"Goodbye, Bea," said Rachel. "I hope we'll see you again soon."

"We'll always be around when our festivals need us," said Bea.

She waved her wand, and each girl found a small, golden candle in her hand. They were flickering with a lustrous yellow flame.

"These are magical candles," Bea said. "Keep them safe and they will burn on every festival day to help you remember us."

"Thank you," said the girls together.

"Goodbye, my friends," said Bea, fluttering upwards into the blue sky. "Goodbye!"

The girls waved until Bea was a tiny speck among the clouds. Then they shared a happy hug.

"Bea's right," said Kirsty. "Happiness does come from helping others."

Emma waved to them from the doorway of the honey-coloured house.

Several people had gathered there, and they were all holding candles.

"We're about to start the march," she said. "I see you have your candles already. Be careful holding them."

Rachel and Kirsty joined her, holding up their candles with everyone else. As the march began, they looked up into

the sky. Somewhere out of sight, they knew that the Buddha Day Fairy was watching over them.

"Goodbye, Bea," they whispered. "Happy Buddha Day!"

The End

Now it's time for Kirsty and Rachel to help ...

Jude the Librarian Fairy

Read on for a sneak peek ...

"Today's the day!" said Kirsty, bouncing out of bed. "Wetherbury's brand-new library is opening at last. Wake up, sleepyhead!"

She jumped on top of the mound of blankets on the spare bed. The mound gave a squeal of laughter and her best friend Rachel Walker sat up.

"I don't need an alarm clock with you around," she said, grinning.

Just then, Kirsty's mum came in with a pile of clean clothes.

"Good morning, girls," she said. "Please get dressed and come downstairs. Dad's cooking a splendid breakfast to make sure that you will have lots of energy to enjoy your big day."

"Thanks, Mum," said Kirsty. "It's a big day for everyone."

"That's true," said Mrs Tate, as she put the clothes away. "I think that almost everyone in the village did something to help raise money for the new library."

Read Jude the Librarian Fairy to find out what adventures are in store for Kirsty and Rachel!

RAINBOW magic

Calling all parents, carers and teachers!
The Rainbow Magic fairies are here to help
your child enter the magical world of reading.
Whatever reading stage they are at, there's
a Rainbow Magic book for everyone!
Here is Lydia the Reading Fairy's guide to
supporting your child's journey at all levels.

Starting Out

Our Rainbow Magic Beginner Readers are perfect for first-time readers who are just beginning to develop reading skills and confidence. Approved by teachers, they contain a full range of educational levelling, as well as lively full-colour illustrations.

Developing Readers

Rainbow Magic Early Readers contain longer stories and wider vocabulary for building stamina and growing confidence. These are adaptations of our most popular Rainbow Magic stories, specially developed for younger readers in conjunction with an Early Years reading consultant, with full-colour illustrations.

Going Solo

The Rainbow Magic chapter books – a mixture of series and one-off specials – contain accessible writing to encourage your child to venture into reading independently. These highly collectible and much-loved magical stories inspire a love of reading to last a lifetime.

www.orchardseriesbooks.co.uk

"Rainbow Magic got my daughter reading chapter books. Great sparkly covers, cute fairies and traditional stories full of magic that she found impossible to put down" – Mother of Edie (6 years)

"Florence LOVES the Rainbow Magic books. She really enjoys reading now" – Mother of Florence (6 years)

Read along the Reading Rainbow!

Well done – you have completed the book!

This book was worth 1 star.

See how far you have climbed on the Reading Rainbow opposite.
The more books you read, the more stars you can colour in
and the closer you will be to becoming a Royal Fairy!

Do you want to print your own Reading Rainbow?

1) Go to the Rainbow Magic website

2) Download and print out the poster

3) Colour in a star for every book you finish
and climb the Reading Rainbow

4) For every step up the rainbow,
you can download your very own certificate

There's all this and lots more at
orchardseriesbooks.co.uk

You'll find activities, stories, a special newsletter
AND you can search for the fairy with your name!